Blue Makes Breakfast

Published by Advance Publishers, L.C.
www.advance-publishers.com

Written by K. Emily Hutta
Art layout by Niall Harding
Art composition by Brad McMahon
Produced by Bumpy Slide Books

ISBN: 1-57973-070-1

Blue's Clues Discovery Series

Oh! Hi! We're glad you're here! It's almost time for our morning cooking lesson with Mr. Salt and Mrs. Pepper.

I'm so excited! We're going to learn how to make some of our favorite breakfast foods today. And then we get to eat them! Hey! Would you like to help? You would? Let's go!

Blue knows something she wants to make for breakfast, and she wants us to play Blue's Clues to figure it out. Will you help me look for Blue's pawprints on three clues? You will? Great!

Cereal with fruit? Yummm. So what do you think we need? Cereal. Right! Can't do without that. And fruit. Yeah. Do you see the fruit? Oh! Blueberries! Good job.

So where should we put the cereal and fruit? In a bowl! Good thinking. I think we need a spoon, too. Anything else? Oh! Milk! The last ingredient! Hey, you're really good at this!

Good idea! Do you see a clue? Where?
Oh! The mixing bowl! So what do you think Blue
wants to make for breakfast using a mixing bowl?
Hmmm. Maybe we'd better find two more clues.

Cool! What do you like on your bagel? Jam and butter? Cream cheese? Peanut butter? They all sound good! I'm really getting hungry now!

Aha! It's a banana. So what do you think Blue wants to make for breakfast using a mixing bowl and a banana? We still need one more clue and then we can figure it out.

We'd better get busy making the fruit salad. Uh-oh. These recipe cards are all mixed up. Can you help me put them in the right order? Thanks!

So what comes first? Taking out the fruit we are going to use. Good thinking. Then what? Oh. Then you wash the fruit. Great! Then you put the cut-up fruit into a bowl. Yeah. And mix it. Good job!

This fruit salad looks delicious! Thanks for helping with the recipe. What's that? You see a clue? Where? Oh! The muffin tin. The muffin tin is our last clue! Wow! You know what that means. It's time to go to our . . . Thinking Chair!

Hmmmm. So what could Blue want to make for breakfast with a mixing bowl, a banana, and a muffin tin? Do you know?

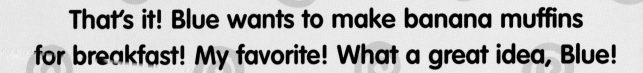

That's it! Blue wants to make banana muffins for breakfast! My favorite! What a great idea, Blue!

Ooh-la-la! What a delicious idea, Blue! And I have the perfect recipe.

Thanks! What should we do first?
Oh! Of course! Read the recipe.
Then . . . hmmm. Oh! We'll
gather together all the
ingredients. Then we'll
follow the directions
very carefully.

Great! What should we do now? Yeah! Let's clean up the kitchen and put everything away. Maybe by the time we're finished, our muffins will be done.

Good idea. So what is missing from our table? Do you know?

Thanks, Mr. Salt and Mrs. Pepper, for showing us how to make this great food. And thank you for helping with Blue's Clues. You're so smart. And I'm soooo hungry. Let's eat!

BLUE'S BANANA MUFFINS*

3 large bananas   **1-1/2 cups flour**   **1 cup brown sugar**

1 tsp.

1 tsp. vanilla

1 tsp.

1 tsp. baking soda

1/2 cup butter   **2 eggs**   **1/4 cup sour cream**   **1/4 tsp. salt**

1-1/2 tsp

1-1/2 tsp. baking powder

1. Preheat oven to 350 degrees.

2. Cream together butter and sugar.

3. Add sour cream, eggs, mashed bananas, and vanilla.

4. Mix all dry ingredients and add to mixture.

5. Pour batter into greased muffin tins (or line with muffin cups).

6. Bake for 20-30 minutes until muffins are golden brown and spring back to the touch. Enjoy!

*Before you start any baking project, ask a grown-up to help you.